'SHE FELT A COZY
SOLIDARITY
WITH THE BIG
COMPANY OF
THE VOLUNTARY
DEAD.'

DOROTHY PARKER
Born 1893, Long Branch, New Jersey, USA
Died 1967, New York City, New York State, USA

All stories taken from *The Collected Dorothy Parker*, first
published in 1944 as *The Portable Dorothy Parker*.

PARKER IN PENGUIN MODERN CLASSICS
The Collected Dorothy Parker

DOROTHY PARKER

The Custard Heart

PENGUIN BOOKS

PENGUIN CLASSICS

UK | USA | Canada | Ireland | Australia
India | New Zealand | South Africa

Penguin Books is part of the Penguin Random House group
of companies whose addresses can be found at
global.penguinrandomhouse.com.

Penguin
Random House
UK

This selection first published 2018
001

Set in 10.25/12.75 pt Dante MT Std
Typeset by Jouve (UK), Milton Keynes
Printed in Great Britain by Clays Ltd, St Ives plc

ISBN: 978-0-241-33958-9

www.greenpenguin.co.uk

MIX
Paper from
responsible sources
FSC® C018179

Penguin Random House is committed to a
sustainable future for our business, our readers
and our planet. This book is made from Forest
Stewardship Council® certified paper.

Contents

The Custard Heart

No living eye, of human being or caged wild beast or dear, domestic animal, had beheld Mrs Lanier when she was not being wistful. She was dedicated to wistfulness, as lesser artists to words and paint and marble. Mrs Lanier was not of the lesser; she was of the true. Surely the eternal example of the true artist is Dickens's actor who blacked himself all over to play Othello. It is safe to assume that Mrs Lanier was wistful in her bathroom, and slumbered soft in wistfulness through the dark and secret night.

If nothing should happen to the portrait of her by Sir James Weir, there she will stand, wistful for the ages. He has shown her at her full length, all in yellows, the delicately heaped curls, the slender, arched feet like elegant bananas, the shining stretch of the evening gown; Mrs Lanier habitually wore white in the evening, but white is the devil's own hue to paint, and could a man be expected to spend his entire six weeks in the States on the execution of a single commission? Wistfulness rests, immortal, in the eyes dark with sad hope, in the pleading mouth, the droop of the little head on the sweet long neck, bowed as if in submission to the three ropes of Lanier pearls. It is true that, when the portrait was exhibited, one critic expressed in print his puzzlement as to what a woman who owned such pearls had to be wistful about; but that was doubtless because he had sold his saffron-colored soul for a few pennies to the proprietor of a rival gallery. Certainly, no man could touch Sir James on pearls. Each one is as distinct, as individual as is each little soldier's face in a Meissonier battle scene.

For a time, with the sitter's obligation to resemble the portrait, Mrs Lanier wore yellow of evenings. She had gowns of velvet like poured country cream and satin with the lacquer of buttercups and chiffon that spiraled about her like golden smoke. She wore them, and listened in shy surprise to the resulting comparisons to daffodils, and butterflies in the sunshine, and such; but she knew.

'It just isn't me,' she sighed at last, and returned to her lily draperies. Picasso had his blue period, and Mrs Lanier her yellow one. They both knew when to stop.

In the afternoons, Mrs Lanier wore black, thin and fragrant, with the great pearls weeping on her breast. What her attire was by morning, only Gwennie, the maid who brought her breakfast tray, could know; but it must, of course, have been exquisite. Mr Lanier – certainly there was a Mr Lanier; he had even been seen – stole past her door on his way out to his office, and the servants glided and murmured, so that Mrs Lanier might be spared as long as possible from the bright new cruelty of the day. Only when the littler, kinder hours had succeeded noon could she bring herself to come forth and face the recurrent sorrows of living.

There was duty to be done, almost daily, and Mrs Lanier made herself brave for it. She must go in her town car to select new clothes and to have fitted to her perfection those she had ordered before. Such garments as hers did not just occur; like great poetry, they required labor. But she shrank from leaving the shelter of her house, for everywhere without were the unlovely and the sad, to assail her eyes and her heart. Often she stood shrinking for several minutes by the baroque mirror in her hall before she could manage to hold her head high and brave, and go on.

There is no safety for the tender, no matter how straight their route, how innocent their destination. Sometimes, even in front of Mrs Lanier's dressmaker's or her furrier's or her lingère's or her milliner's, there would be a file of thin girls and small, shabby men, who held placards in their cold hands and paced up and down and up and down with slow, measured steps. Their faces would be blue and rough from the wind, and blank with the monotony of their treadmill. They looked so little and poor and strained that Mrs Lanier's hands would fly to her heart in pity. Her eyes would be luminous with sympathy and her sweet lips would part as if on a whisper of cheer, as she passed through the draggled line into the shop.

Often there would be pencil-sellers in her path, a half of a creature set upon a sort of roller-skate thrusting himself along the pavement by his hand or a blind man shuffling after his wavering cane. Mrs Lanier must stop and sway, her eyes closed, one hand about her throat to support her lovely, stricken head. Then you could actually see her force herself, could see the

3

effort ripple her body, as she opened her eyes and gave these miserable ones, the blind and the seeing alike, a smile of such tenderness, such sorrowful understanding, that it was like the exquisite sad odor of hyacinths on the air. Sometimes, if the man was not too horrible, she could even reach in her purse for a coin and, holding it as lightly as if she had plucked it from a silvery stem, extend her slim arm and drop it in his cup. If he was young and new at his life, he would offer her pencils for the worth of her money; but Mrs Lanier wanted no returns. In gentlest delicacy she would slip away, leaving him with mean wares intact, not a worker for his livelihood like a million others, but signal and set apart, rare in the fragrance of charity.

So it was, when Mrs Lanier went out. Everywhere she saw them, the ragged, the wretched, the desperate, and to each she gave her look that spoke with no words.

'Courage,' it said. 'And you – oh, wish me courage, too!'

Frequently, by the time she returned to her house, Mrs Lanier would be limp as a freesia. Her maid Gwennie would have to beseech her to lie down, to gain the strength to change her gown for a filmier one and descend to her drawing-room, her eyes darkly mournful, but her exquisite breasts pointed high.

In her drawing-room, there was sanctuary. Here her heart might heal from the blows of the world, and be whole for its own sorrow. It was a room suspended above life, a place of tender fabrics and pale flowers, with never a paper or a book to report the harrowing or describe it. Below the great sheet of its window swung the river, and the stately scows went by laden with strange stuff in rich tapestry colors; there was no necessity to belong to the sort who must explain that it was garbage. An island with a happy name lay opposite, and on it stood a row of prim, tight buildings, naive as a painting by Rousseau. Sometimes there could be seen on the island the brisk figures of nurses and internes, sporting in the lanes. Possibly there were figures considerably less brisk beyond the barred windows of the buildings, but that was not to be wondered about in the presence of Mrs Lanier. All those who came to her drawing-room came in one cause, to shield her heart from hurt.

Here in her drawing-room, in the lovely blue of the late day, Mrs Lanier sat upon opalescent taffeta and was wistful. And here to her drawing-room, the young men came and tried to help her bear her life.

There was a pattern to the visits of the young men. They would come in groups of three or four or six, for a while; and then there would be one of them who would stay a little after the rest had gone, who presently would come a little earlier than the others. Then there would be days when Mrs Lanier would cease to be at home to the other young men, and that one young man would be alone with her in the lovely blue. And then Mrs Lanier would no longer be at home to that one young man, and Gwennie would have to tell him and tell him, over the telephone, that Mrs Lanier was out, that Mrs Lanier was ill, that Mrs Lanier could not be disturbed. The groups of young men would come again; that one young man would not be with them. But there would be, among them, a new young man, who presently would stay a little later and come a little earlier, who eventually would plead with Gwennie over the telephone.

Gwennie – her widowed mother had named her Gwendola, and then, as if realizing that no other dream would ever come true, had died – was little and compact and unnoticeable. She had been raised on an upstate farm by an uncle and aunt hard as the soil they fought for their lives. After their deaths, she had no relatives anywhere. She came to New York, because she had heard stories of jobs; her arrival was at the time when Mrs Lanier's cook needed a kitchen-maid. So in her own house, Mrs Lanier had found her treasure.

Gwennie's hard little farm-girl's fingers could set invisible stitches, could employ a flatiron as if it were a wand, could be as summer breezes in the robing of Mrs Lanier and the tending of her hair. She was as busy as the day was long; and her days frequently extended from daybreak to daybreak. She was never tired, she had no grievance, she was cheerful without being expressive about it. There was nothing in her presence or the sight of her to touch the heart and thus cause discomfort.

Mrs Lanier would often say that she didn't know what she would do without her little Gwennie; if her little Gwennie should ever leave her, she said, she just couldn't go on. She looked so lorn and fragile as she said it that one scowled upon Gwennie for the potentialities of death or marriage that the girl carried within her. Yet there was no pressing cause for worry, for Gwennie was strong as a pony and had no beau. She had made no friends at all, and seemed not to observe the omission. Her life was for Mrs Lanier; like all others who were permitted close, Gwennie sought to do what she could to save Mrs Lanier from pain.

They could all assist in shutting out reminders of the sadness abroad in the world, but Mrs Lanier's private sorrow was a more difficult matter. There dwelt a yearning so deep, so secret in her heart that it would often be days before she could speak of it, in the twilight, to a new young man.

'If I only had a little baby,' she would sigh, 'a little, little baby, I think I could be almost happy.' And she would fold her delicate arms, and lightly, slowly rock them, as if they cradled that little, little one of her dear dreams. Then, the denied madonna, she was at her most wistful, and the young man would have lived or died for her, as she bade him.

Mrs Lanier never mentioned why her wish was unfulfilled; the young man would know her to be too sweet to place blame, too proud to tell. But, so close to her in the pale light, he would understand, and his blood would swirl with fury that such clods as Mr Lanier remained unkilled. He would beseech Mrs Lanier, first in halting murmurs, then in rushes of hot words, to let him take her away from the hell of her life and try to make her almost happy. It would be after this that Mrs Lanier would be out to the young man, would be ill, would be incapable of being disturbed.

Gwennie did not enter the drawing-room when there was only one young man there; but when the groups returned she served unobtrusively, drawing a curtain or fetching a fresh glass. All the Lanier servants were unobtrusive, light of step and correctly indistinct of feature. When there must be changes made in the staff, Gwennie and the housekeeper arranged the replacements and did not speak of the matter to Mrs Lanier, lest she should be stricken by desertions or saddened by tales of woe. Always the new servants resembled the old, alike in that they were unnoticeable. That is, until Kane, the new chauffeur, came.

The old chauffeur had been replaced because he had been the old chauffeur too long. It weighs cruelly heavy on the tender heart when a familiar face grows lined and dry, when familiar shoulders seem daily to droop lower, a familiar nape is hollow between cords. The old chauffeur saw and heard and functioned with no difference; but it was too much for Mrs Lanier to see what was befalling him. With pain in her voice, she had told Gwennie that she could stand the sight of him no longer. So the old chauffeur had gone, and Kane had come.

Kane was young, and there was nothing depressing about his straight shoulders and his firm, full neck to one sitting behind them in the town car. He stood, a fine triangle in his fitted uniform, holding the door of the car open for Mrs Lanier and bowed his head as she passed. But when he was not at work, his head was held high and slightly cocked, and there was a little cocked smile on his red mouth.

Often, in the cold weather when Kane waited for her in the car, Mrs Lanier would humanely bid Gwennie to tell him to come in and wait in the servants' sitting-room. Gwennie brought him coffee and looked at him. Twice she did not hear Mrs Lanier's enameled electric bell.

Gwennie began to observe her evenings off; before, she had disregarded them and stayed to minister to Mrs Lanier. There was one night when Mrs Lanier had floated late to her room, after a theater and a long conversation, done in murmurs, in the drawing-room. And Gwennie had not been waiting, to take off the white gown, and put away the pearls, and brush the bright hair that curled like the petals of forsythia. Gwennie had not yet returned to the house from her holiday. Mrs Lanier had had to arouse a parlor-maid and obtain unsatisfactory aid from her.

Gwennie had wept, next morning, at the pathos of Mrs Lanier's eyes; but tears were too distressing for Mrs Lanier to see, and the girl stopped them. Mrs Lanier delicately patted her arm, and there had been nothing more of the matter, save that Mrs Lanier's eyes were darker and wider for this new hurt.

Kane became a positive comfort to Mrs Lanier. After the sorry sights of the streets, it was good to see Kane standing by the car, solid and straight and young, with nothing in the world the trouble with him. Mrs Lanier came to smile upon him almost gratefully, yet wistfully, too, as if she would seek of him the secret of not being sad.

And then, one day, Kane did not appear at his appointed time. The car, which should have been waiting to convey Mrs Lanier to her dressmaker's, was still in the garage, and Kane had not appeared there all day. Mrs Lanier told Gwennie immediately to telephone the place where he roomed and find out what this meant. The girl had cried out at her, cried out that she had called and called and called, and he was not there and no one there knew where he was. The crying out must have been due to Gwennie's loss of head in her distress at this disruption of Mrs Lanier's day; or perhaps it was the effect on her voice of an appalling cold she seemed to have contracted, for her eyes were heavy and red and her face pale and swollen.

There was no more of Kane. He had had his wages paid him on the day before he disappeared, and that was the last of him. There was never a word and not another sight of him. At first, Mrs Lanier could scarcely bring herself to believe that such betrayal could exist. Her heart, soft and sweet as a perfectly made *crème renversée*, quivered in her breast, and in her eyes lay the far light of suffering.

'Oh, how could he do this to me?' she asked piteously of Gwennie. 'How could he do this to poor me?'

There was no discussion of the defection of Kane; it was too painful a subject. If a caller heedlessly asked whatever had become of that nice-looking chauffeur, Mrs Lanier would lay her hand over her closed lids and slowly wince. The caller would be suicidal that he had thus unconsciously added to her sorrows, and would strive his consecrated best to comfort her.

Gwennie's cold lasted for an extraordinarily long time. The weeks went by, and still, every morning, her eyes were red and her face white and puffed. Mrs Lanier often had to look away from her when she brought the breakfast tray.

She tended Mrs Lanier as carefully as ever; she gave no attention to her holidays, but stayed to do further service. She had always been quiet, and she became all but silent, and that was additionally soothing. She worked without stopping and seemed to thrive, for, save for the effects of the curious cold, she looked round and healthy.

'See,' Mrs Lanier said in tender raillery, as the girl attended the group in the drawing-room, 'see how fat my little Gwennie's getting! Isn't that cute?'

The weeks went on, and the pattern of the young men shifted again. There came the day when Mrs Lanier was not at home to a group; when a new young man was to come and be alone with her, for his first time, in the drawing-room. Mrs Lanier sat before her mirror and lightly touched her throat with perfume, while Gwennie heaped the golden curls.

The exquisite face Mrs Lanier saw in the mirror drew her closer attention, and she put down the perfume and leaned toward it. She drooped her head a little to the side and watched it closely; she saw the wistful eyes grow yet more wistful, the lips curve to a pleading smile. She folded her arms close to her sweet breast and slowly rocked them, as if they cradled a dream-child. She watched the mirrored arms sway gently, caused them to sway a little slower.

'If I only had a little baby,' she sighed. She shook her head. Delicately she cleared her throat, and sighed again on a slightly lower note. 'If I only had a little, little baby, I think I could be almost happy.'

There was a clatter from behind her, and she turned, amazed. Gwennie had dropped the hair-brush to the floor and stood swaying, with her face in her hands.

'Gwennie!' said Mrs Lanier. 'Gwennie!'

The girl took her hands from her face, and it was as if she stood under a green light.

'I'm sorry,' she panted. 'Sorry. Please excuse me. I'm – oh, I'm going to be sick!'

She ran from the room so violently that the floor shook.

Mrs Lanier sat looking after Gwennie, her hands at her wounded heart. Slowly she turned back to her mirror, and what she saw there arrested her; the artist knows the masterpiece. Here was the perfection of her career, the sublimation of wistfulness; it was that look of grieved bewilderment that did it. Carefully she kept it upon her face as she rose from the mirror and, with her lovely hands still shielding her heart, went down to the new young man.

Big Blonde

Hazel Morse was a large, fair woman of the type that incites some men when they use the word 'blonde' to click their tongues and wag their heads roguishly. She prided herself upon her small feet and suffered for her vanity, boxing them in snub-toed, high-heeled slippers of the shortest bearable size. The curious things about her were her hands, strange termin-ations to the flabby white arms splattered with pale tan spots – long, quivering hands with deep and convex nails. She should not have disfigured them with little jewels.

She was not a woman given to recollections. At her middle thirties, her old days were a blurred and flickering sequence, an imperfect film, dealing with the actions of strangers.

In her twenties, after the deferred death of a hazy widowed mother, she had been employed as a model in a wholesale dress establishment – it was still the day of the big woman, and she was then prettily colored and erect and high-breasted. Her job was not onerous, and she met numbers of men and spent numbers of evenings with them, laughing at their jokes and telling them she loved their neckties. Men liked her, and she took it for granted that the liking of many men was a desirable thing. Popularity seemed to her to be worth all the

13

work that had to be put into its achievement. Men liked you because you were fun, and when they liked you they took you out, and there you were. So, and successfully, she was fun. She was a good sport. Men liked a good sport.

No other form of diversion, simpler or more complicated, drew her attention. She never pondered if she might not be better occupied doing something else. Her ideas, or, better, her acceptances, ran right along with those of the other substantially built blondes in whom she found her friends.

When she had been working in the dress establishment some years she met Herbie Morse. He was thin, quick, attractive, with shifting lines about his shiny, brown eyes and a habit of fiercely biting at the skin around his finger nails. He drank largely: she found that entertaining. Her habitual greeting to him was an allusion to his state of the previous night.

'Oh, what a peach you had,' she used to say, through her easy laugh. 'I thought I'd die, the way you kept asking the waiter to dance with you.'

She liked him immediately upon their meeting. She was enormously amused at his fast, slurred sentences, his interpolations of apt phrases from vaudeville acts and comic strips; she thrilled at the feel of his lean arm tucked firm beneath the sleeve of her coat; she wanted to touch the wet, flat surface of his hair. He was as promptly drawn to her. They were married six weeks after they had met.

She was delighted at the idea of being a bride; coquetted with it, played upon it. Other offers of marriage she had had, and not a few of them, but it happened that they were all from stout, serious men who had visited the dress establishment as buyers; men from Des Moines and Houston and Chicago and, in her phrase, even funnier places. There was always something immensely comic to her in the thought of living elsewhere than New York. She could not regard as serious proposals that she share a western residence.

She wanted to be married. She was nearing thirty now, and she did not take the years well. She spread and softened, and her darkening hair turned her to inexpert dabblings with peroxide. There were times when she had little flashes of fear about her job. And she had had a couple of thousand evenings of being a good sport among her male acquaintances. She had come to be more conscientious than spontaneous about it.

Herbie earned enough, and they took a little apartment far uptown. There was a Mission-furnished dining-room with a hanging central light globed in liver-colored glass; in the living-room were an 'over-stuffed suite,' a Boston fern, and a reproduction of the Henner 'Magdalene' with the red hair and the blue draperies; the bedroom was in gray enamel and old rose, with Herbie's photograph on Hazel's dressing-table and Hazel's likeness on Herbie's chest of drawers.

She cooked – and she was a good cook – and marketed and chatted with the delivery boys and the colored laundress. She loved the flat, she loved her life, she loved Herbie. In the first months of their marriage, she gave him all the passion she was ever to know.

She had not realized how tired she was. It was a delight, a new game, a holiday, to give up being a good sport. If her head ached or her arches throbbed, she complained piteously, baby-ishly. If her mood was quiet, she did not talk. If tears came to her eyes, she let them fall.

She fell readily into the habit of tears during the first year of her marriage. Even in her good sport days, she had been known to weep lavishly and disinterestedly on occasion. Her behavior at the theater was a standing joke. She could weep at anything in a play – tiny garments, love both unrequited and mutual, seduction, purity, faithful servitors, wedlock, the triangle.

'There goes Haze,' her friends would say, watching her. 'She's off again.'

Wedded and relaxed, she poured her tears freely. To her who had laughed so much, crying was delicious. All sorrows became her sorrows; she was Tenderness. She would cry long and softly over newspaper accounts of kidnaped babies, deserted wives, unemployed men, strayed cats, heroic dogs. Even when the paper was no longer before her, her mind revolved upon these things and the drops slipped rhythmically over her plump cheeks.

'Honestly,' she would say to Herbie, 'all the sadness there is in the world when you stop to think about it!'

'Yeah,' Herbie would say.

She missed nobody. The old crowd, the people who had brought her and Herbie together, dropped from their lives, lingeringly at first. When she thought of this at all, it was only to consider it fitting. This was marriage. This was peace.

But the thing was that Herbie was not amused.

For a time, he had enjoyed being alone with her. He found the voluntary isolation novel and sweet. Then it palled with a ferocious suddenness. It was as if one night, sitting with her in the steam-heated living-room, he would ask no more; and the next night he was through and done with the whole thing.

He became annoyed by her misty melancholies. At first, when he came home to find her softly tired and moody, he kissed her neck and patted her shoulder and begged her to tell her Herbie what was wrong. She loved that. But time slid by, and he found that there was never anything really, personally, the matter.

'Ah, for God's sake,' he would say. 'Crabbing again. All right, sit here and crab your head off. I'm going out.'

And he would slam out of the flat and come back late and drunk.

She was completely bewildered by what happened to their marriage. First they were lovers; and then, it seemed without transition, they were enemies. She never understood it.

There were longer and longer intervals between his leaving his office and his arrival at the apartment. She went through agonies of picturing him run over and bleeding, dead and covered with a sheet. Then she lost her fears for his safety and grew sullen and wounded. When a person wanted to be with a person, he came as soon as possible. She desperately wanted him to want to be with her; her own hours only marked the time till he would come. It was often nearly nine o'clock before he came home to dinner. Always he had had many drinks, and their effect would die in him, leaving him loud and querulous and bristling for affronts.

He was too nervous, he said, to sit and do nothing for an evening. He boasted, probably not in all truth, that he had never read a book in his life.

'What am I expected to do – sit around this dump on my tail all night?' he would ask, rhetorically. And again he would slam out.

She did not know what to do. She could not manage him. She could not meet him.

She fought him furiously. A terrific domesticity had come upon her, and she would bite and scratch to guard it. She wanted what she called 'a nice home.' She wanted a sober, tender husband, prompt at dinner, punctual at work. She wanted sweet, comforting evenings. The idea of intimacy with other men was terrible to her; the thought that Herbie might be seeking entertainment in other women set her frantic.

It seemed to her that almost everything she read – novels from the drug-store lending library, magazine stories, women's pages in the papers – dealt with wives who lost their husbands' love. She could bear those, at that, better than accounts of neat, companionable marriage and living happily ever after.

She was frightened. Several times when Herbie came home in the evening, he found her determinedly dressed – she had had to alter those of her clothes that were not new, to make them fasten – and rouged.

'Let's go wild tonight, what do you say?' she would hail

him. 'A person's got lots of time to hang around and do nothing when they're dead.'

So they would go out, to chop houses and the less expensive cabarets. But it turned out badly. She could no longer find amusement in watching Herbie drink. She could not laugh at his whimsicalities, she was so tensely counting his indulgences. And she was unable to keep back her remonstrances – 'Ah, come on, Herb, you've had enough, haven't you? You'll feel something terrible in the morning.'

He would be immediately enraged. All right, crab; crab, crab, crab, crab, that was all she ever did. What a lousy sport *she* was! There would be scenes, and one or the other of them would rise and stalk out in fury.

She could not recall the definite day that she started drinking, herself. There was nothing separate about her days. Like drops upon a window-pane, they ran together and trickled away. She had been married six months; then a year; then three years.

She had never needed to drink, formerly. She could sit for most of a night at a table where the others were imbibing earnestly and never droop in looks or spirits, nor be bored by the doings of those about her. If she took a cocktail, it was so unusual as to cause twenty minutes or so of jocular comment. But now anguish was in her. Frequently, after a quarrel, Herbie would stay out for the night, and she could not learn from him where the time had been spent. Her heart felt tight and sore in her breast, and her mind turned like an electric fan.

She hated the taste of liquor. Gin, plain or in mixtures, made her promptly sick. After experiment, she found that Scotch whisky was best for her. She took it without water, because that was the quickest way to its effect.

Herbie pressed it on her. He was glad to see her drink. They both felt it might restore her high spirits, and their good times together might again be possible.

''Atta girl,' he would approve her. 'Let's see you get boiled, baby.'

But it brought them no nearer. When she drank with him, there would be a little while of gaiety and then, strangely without beginning, they would be in a wild quarrel. They would wake in the morning not sure what it had all been about, foggy as to what had been said and done, but each deeply injured and bitterly resentful. There would be days of vengeful silence.

There had been a time when they had made up their quarrels, usually in bed. There would be kisses and little names and assurances of fresh starts . . . 'Oh, it's going to be great now, Herb. We'll have swell times. I was a crab. I guess I must have been tired. But everything's going to be swell. You'll see.'

Now there were no gentle reconciliations. They resumed friendly relations only in the brief magnanimity caused by liquor, before more liquor drew them into new battles. The scenes became more violent. There were shouted invectives and pushes, and sometimes sharp slaps. Once she had a black eye. Herbie was horrified next day at the sight of it. He did not go to work; he followed her about, suggesting remedies and heaping dark blame on himself. But after they had had a few drinks – 'to pull themselves together' – she made so many wistful references to her bruise that he shouted at her and rushed out and was gone for two days.

Each time he left the place in a rage, he threatened never to come back. She did not believe him, nor did she consider separation. Somewhere in her head or her heart was the lazy, nebulous hope that things would change and she and Herbie settle suddenly into soothing married life. Here were her home, her furniture, her husband, her station. She summoned no alternatives.

She could no longer bustle and potter. She had no more vicarious tears; the hot drops she shed were for herself. She walked ceaselessly about the rooms, her thoughts running mechanically round and round Herbie. In those days began the hatred of being alone that she was never to overcome. You could be by yourself when things were all right, but when you were blue you got the howling horrors.

She commenced drinking alone, little, short drinks all through the day. It was only with Herbie that alcohol made her nervous and quick in offense. Alone, it blurred sharp things for her. She lived in a haze of it. Her life took on a dream-like quality. Nothing was astonishing.

A Mrs Martin moved into the flat across the hall. She was a great blonde woman of forty, a promise in looks of what Mrs Morse was to be. They made acquaintance, quickly became inseparable. Mrs Morse spent her days in the opposite apartment. They drank together, to brace themselves after the drinks of the nights before.

She never confided her troubles about Herbie to Mrs Martin. The subject was too bewildering to her to find comfort in talk. She let it be assumed that her husband's business kept him much away. It was not regarded as important; husbands, as such, played but shadowy parts in Mrs Martin's circle.

Mrs Martin had no visible spouse; you were left to decide for yourself whether he was or was not dead. She had an admirer, Joe, who came to see her almost nightly. Often he brought several friends with him – 'The Boys,' they were called. The Boys were big, red, good-humored men, perhaps forty-five, perhaps fifty. Mrs Morse was glad of invitations to join the parties – Herbie was scarcely ever at home at night now. If he did come home, she did not visit Mrs Martin. An evening alone with Herbie meant inevitably a quarrel, yet she would stay with him. There was always her thin and wordless idea that, maybe, this night, things would begin to be all right.

The Boys brought plenty of liquor along with them whenever they came to Mrs Martin's. Drinking with them, Mrs Morse became lively and good-natured and audacious. She was quickly popular. When she had drunk enough to cloud her most recent battle with Herbie, she was excited by their approbation. Crab, was she? Rotten sport, was she? Well, there were some that thought different.

Ed was one of The Boys. He lived in Utica – had 'his own business' there, was the awed report – but he came to New York almost every week. He was married. He showed Mrs Morse the then current photographs of Junior and Sister, and she praised them abundantly and sincerely. Soon it was accepted by the others that Ed was her particular friend.

He staked her when they all played poker; sat next to her and occasionally rubbed his knee against hers during the game. She was rather lucky. Frequently she went home with a twenty-dollar bill or a ten-dollar bill or a handful of crumpled dollars. She was glad of them. Herbie was getting, in her words, something awful about money. To ask him for it brought an instant row.

'What the hell do you do with it?' he would say. 'Shoot it all on Scotch?'

'I try to run this house half-way decent,' she would retort. 'Never thought of that, did you? Oh, no, his lordship couldn't be bothered with that.'

Again, she could not find a definite day, to fix the beginning of Ed's proprietorship. It became his custom to kiss her on the mouth when he came in, as well as for farewell, and he gave her little quick kisses of approval all through the evening. She liked this rather more than she disliked it. She never thought of his kisses when she was not with him.

He would run his hand lingeringly over her back and shoulders.

'Some dizzy blonde, eh?' he would say. 'Some doll.'

One afternoon she came home from Mrs Martin's to find Herbie in the bedroom. He had been away for several nights, evidently on a prolonged drinking bout. His face was gray, his hands jerked as if they were on wires. On the bed were two old suitcases, packed high. Only her photograph remained on his bureau, and the wide doors of his closet disclosed nothing but coat-hangers.

'I'm blowing,' he said. 'I'm through with the whole works. I got a job in Detroit.'

She sat down on the edge of the bed. She had drunk much the night before, and the four Scotches she had had with Mrs Martin had only increased her fogginess.

'Good job?' she said.

'Oh, yeah,' he said. 'Looks all right.'

He closed a suitcase with difficulty, swearing at it in whispers.

'There's some dough in the bank,' he said. 'The bank book's in your top drawer. You can have the furniture and stuff.'

He looked at her, and his forehead twitched.

'God damn it, I'm through, I'm telling you,' he cried. 'I'm through.'

'All right, all right,' she said. 'I heard you, didn't I?'

She saw him as if he were at one end of a cannon and she at the other. Her head was beginning to ache bumpingly, and her voice had a dreary, tiresome tone. She could not have raised it.

'Like a drink before you go?' she asked.

Again he looked at her, and a corner of his mouth jerked up.

'Cockeyed again for a change, aren't you?' he said. 'That's nice. Sure, get a couple of shots, will you?'

She went to the pantry, mixed him a stiff highball, poured herself a couple of inches of whisky and drank it. Then she gave herself another portion and brought the glasses into the bedroom. He had strapped both suitcases and had put on his hat and overcoat.

He took his highball.

'Well,' he said, and he gave a sudden, uncertain laugh. 'Here's mud in your eye.'

'Mud in your eye,' she said.

They drank. He put down his glass and took up the heavy suitcases.

'Got to get a train around six,' he said.

She followed him down the hall. There was a song, a song that Mrs Martin played doggedly on the phonograph, running loudly through her mind. She had never liked the thing.

> *Night and daytime,*
> *Always playtime.*
> *Ain't we got fun?*

At the door he put down the bags and faced her.

'Well,' he said. 'Well, take care of yourself. You'll be all right, will you?'

'Oh, sure,' she said.

He opened the door, then came back to her, holding out his hand.

''By, Haze,' he said. 'Good luck to you.'

She took his hand and shook it.

'Pardon my wet glove,' she said.

When the door had closed behind him, she went back to the pantry.

She was flushed and lively when she went in to Mrs Martin's

that evening. The Boys were there, Ed among them. He was glad to be in town, frisky and loud and full of jokes. But she spoke quietly to him for a minute.

'Herbie blew today,' she said. 'Going to live out west.'

'That so?' he said. He looked at her and played with the fountain pen clipped to his waistcoat pocket.

'Think he's gone for good, do you?' he asked.

'Yeah,' she said. 'I know he is. I know. Yeah.'

'You going to live on across the hall just the same?' he said. 'Know what you're going to do?'

'Gee, I don't know,' she said. 'I don't give much of a damn.'

'Oh, come on, that's no way to talk,' he told her. 'What you need – you need a little snifter. How about it?'

'Yeah,' she said. 'Just straight.'

She won forty-three dollars at poker. When the game broke up, Ed took her back to her apartment.

'Got a little kiss for me?' he asked.

He wrapped her in his big arms and kissed her violently. She was entirely passive. He held her away and looked at her.

'Little tight, honey?' he asked, anxiously. 'Not going to be sick, are you?'

'Me?' she said. 'I'm swell.'

I I

When Ed left in the morning, he took her photograph with him. He said he wanted her picture to look at, up in Utica. 'You can have that one on the bureau,' she said.

She put Herbie's picture in a drawer, out of her sight. When she could look at it, she meant to tear it up. She was fairly successful in keeping her mind from racing around him. Whisky slowed it for her. She was almost peaceful, in her mist.

She accepted her relationship with Ed without question or enthusiasm. When he was away, she seldom thought definitely of him. He was good to her; he gave her frequent presents and a regular allowance. She was even able to save. She did not plan ahead of any day, but her wants were few, and you might as well put money in the bank as have it lying around.

When the lease of her apartment neared its end, it was Ed who suggested moving. His friendship with Mrs Martin and Joe had become strained over a dispute at poker; a feud was impending.

'Let's get the hell out of here,' Ed said. 'What I want you to have is a place near the Grand Central. Make it easier for me.'

So she took a little flat in the Forties. A colored maid came in every day to clean and to make coffee for her – she was 'through with that housekeeping stuff,' she said, and Ed, twenty years married to a passionately domestic woman, admired this romantic uselessness and felt doubly a man of the world in abetting it.

The coffee was all she had until she went out to dinner, but alcohol kept her fat. Prohibition she regarded only as a basis for jokes. You could always get all you wanted. She was never noticeably drunk and seldom nearly sober. It required a larger daily allowance to keep her misty-minded. Too little, and she was achingly melancholy.

Ed brought her to Jimmy's. He was proud, with the pride of the transient who would be mistaken for a native, in his knowledge of small, recent restaurants occupying the lower floors of shabby brownstone houses; places where, upon mentioning the name of an habitué friend, might be obtained strange whisky and fresh gin in many of their ramifications. Jimmy's place was the favorite of his acquaintances.

There, through Ed, Mrs Morse met many men and women, formed quick friendships. The men often took her out when Ed was in Utica. He was proud of her popularity.

She fell into the habit of going to Jimmy's alone when she had no engagement. She was certain to meet some people she knew, and join them. It was a club for her friends, both men and women.

The women at Jimmy's looked remarkably alike, and this was curious, for, through feuds, removals, and opportunities of more profitable contacts, the personnel of the group changed constantly. Yet always the newcomers resembled those whom they replaced. They were all big women and stout, broad of shoulder and abundantly breasted, with faces thickly clothed in soft, high-colored flesh. They laughed loud and often, showing opaque and lusterless teeth like squares of crockery. There was about them the health of the big, yet a slight, unwholesome suggestion of stubborn preservation. They might have been thirty-six or forty-five or anywhere between.

They composed their titles of their own first names with their husbands' surnames – Mrs Florence Miller, Mrs Vera Riley, Mrs Lilian Block. This gave at the same time the solidity of marriage and the glamour of freedom. Yet only one or two were actually divorced. Most of them never referred to their dimmed spouses; some, a shorter time separated, described them in terms of great biological interest. Several were mothers, each of an only child – a boy at school somewhere, or a girl being cared for by a grandmother. Often, well on toward morning, there would be displays of kodak portraits and of tears.

They were comfortable women, cordial and friendly and irrepressibly matronly. Theirs was the quality of ease. Become fatalistic, especially about money matters, they unworried. Whenever their funds dropped alarmingly, a new donor appeared; this had always happened. The aim of each was to have one man, permanently, to pay all her bills, in return for which she would have immediately given up other admirers and probably would have become exceedingly fond of him; for the affections of all of them were, by now, unexacting, tranquil, and easily arranged. This end, however, grew increasingly difficult yearly. Mrs Morse was regarded as fortunate.

Ed had a good year, increased her allowance and gave her a sealskin coat. But she had to be careful of her moods with him. He insisted upon gaiety. He would not listen to admissions of aches or weariness.

'Hey, listen,' he would say, 'I got worries of my own, and plenty. Nobody wants to hear other people's troubles, sweetie.

What you got to do, you got to be a sport and forget it. See? Well, slip us a little smile, then. That's my girl.'

She never had enough interest to quarrel with him as she had with Herbie, but she wanted the privilege of occasional admitted sadness. It was strange. The other women she saw did not have to fight their moods. There was Mrs Florence Miller who got regular crying jags, and the men sought only to cheer and comfort her. The others spent whole evenings in grieved recitals of worries and ills; their escorts paid them deep sympathy. But she was instantly undesirable when she was low in spirits. Once, at Jimmy's, when she could not make herself lively, Ed had walked out and left her.

'Why the hell don't you stay home and not go spoiling everybody's evening?' he had roared.

Even her slightest acquaintances seemed irritated if she were not conspicuously light-hearted.

'What's the matter with you, anyway?' they would say. 'Be your age, why don't you? Have a little drink and snap out of it.'

When her relationship with Ed had continued nearly three years, he moved to Florida to live. He hated leaving her; he gave her a large check and some shares of a sound stock, and his pale eyes were wet when he said good-by. She did not miss him. He came to New York infrequently, perhaps two or three times a year, and hurried directly from the train to see her. She was always pleased to have him come and never sorry to see him go.

Charley, an acquaintance of Ed's that she had met at

Jimmy's, had long admired her. He had always made opportunities of touching her and leaning close to talk to her. He
asked repeatedly of all their friends if they had ever heard such
a fine laugh as she had. After Ed left, Charley became the main
figure in her life. She classified him and spoke of him as 'not
so bad.' There was nearly a year of Charley; then she divided
her time between him and Sydney, another frequenter of
Jimmy's; then Charley slipped away altogether.

Sydney was a little, brightly dressed, clever Jew. She was
perhaps nearest contentment with him. He amused her
always; her laughter was not forced.

He admired her completely. Her softness and size delighted
him. And he thought she was great, he often told her, because
she kept gay and lively when she was drunk.

'Once I had a gal,' he said, 'used to try and throw herself
out of the window every time she got a can on. Jee-*zuss*,' he
added, feelingly.

Then Sydney married a rich and watchful bride, and then
there was Billy. No – after Sydney came Fred, then Billy. In her
haze, she never recalled how men entered her life and left it.
There were no surprises. She had no thrill at their advent, nor
woe at their departure. She seemed to be always able to attract
men. There was never another as rich as Ed, but they were all
generous to her, in their means.

Once she had news of Herbie. She met Mrs Martin dining
at Jimmy's, and the old friendship was vigorously renewed.
The still admiring Joe, while on a business trip, had seen Herbie. He had settled in Chicago, he looked fine, he was living

with some woman – seemed to be crazy about her. Mrs Morse had been drinking vastly that day. She took the news with mild interest, as one hearing of the sex peccadilloes of somebody whose name is, after a moment's groping, familiar.

'Must be damn near seven years since I saw him,' she commented. 'Gee. Seven years.'

More and more, her days lost their individuality. She never knew dates, nor was sure of the day of the week.

'My God, was that a year ago!' she would exclaim, when an event was recalled in conversation.

She was tired so much of the time. Tired and blue. Almost everything could give her the blues. Those old horses she saw on Sixth Avenue – struggling and slipping along the car-tracks, or standing at the curb, their heads dropped level with their worn knees. The tightly stored tears would squeeze from her eyes as she teetered past on her aching feet in the stubby, champagne-colored slippers.

The thought of death came and stayed with her and lent her a sort of drowsy cheer. It would be nice, nice and restful, to be dead.

There was no settled, shocked moment when she first thought of killing herself; it seemed to her as if the idea had always been with her. She pounced upon all the accounts of suicides in the newspapers. There was an epidemic of self-killings – or maybe it was just that she searched for the stories of them so eagerly that she found many. To read of them roused reassurance in her; she felt a cozy solidarity with the big company of the voluntary dead.

She slept, aided by whisky, till deep into the afternoons, then lay abed, a bottle and glass at her hand, until it was time to dress and go out for dinner. She was beginning to feel toward alcohol a little puzzled distrust, as toward an old friend who has refused a simple favor. Whisky could still soothe her for most of the time, but there were sudden, inexplicable moments when the cloud fell treacherously away from her, and she was sawed by the sorrow and bewilderment and nuisance of all living. She played voluptuously with the thought of cool, sleepy retreat. She had never been troubled by religious belief and no vision of an after-life intimidated her. She dreamed by day of never again putting on tight shoes, of never having to laugh and listen and admire, of never more being a good sport. Never.

But how would you do it? It made her sick to think of jumping from heights. She could not stand a gun. At the theater, if one of the actors drew a revolver, she crammed her fingers into her ears and could not even look at the stage until after the shot had been fired. There was no gas in her flat. She looked long at the bright blue veins in her slim wrists – a cut with a razor blade, and there you'd be. But it would hurt, hurt like hell, and there would be blood to see. Poison – something tasteless and quick and painless – was the thing. But they wouldn't sell it to you in drug-stores, because of the law.

She had few other thoughts.

There was a new man now – Art. He was short and fat and exacting and hard on her patience when he was drunk. But there had been only occasionals for some time before him, and she was glad of a little stability. Too, Art must be away for weeks at a stretch, selling silks, and that was restful. She was convincingly gay with him, though the effort shook her.

'The best sport in the world,' he would murmur, deep in her neck. 'The best sport in the world.'

One night, when he had taken her to Jimmy's, she went into the dressing-room with Mrs Florence Miller. There, while designing curly mouths on their faces with lip-rouge, they compared experiences of insomnia.

'Honestly,' Mrs Morse said, 'I wouldn't close an eye if I didn't go to bed full of Scotch. I lie there and toss and turn and toss and turn. Blue! Does a person get blue lying awake that way!'

'Say, listen, Hazel,' Mrs Miller said, impressively, 'I'm telling you I'd be awake for a year if I didn't take veronal. That stuff makes you sleep like a fool.'

'Isn't it poison, or something?' Mrs Morse asked.

'Oh, you take too much and you're out for the count,' said Mrs Miller. 'I just take five grains – they come in tablets. I'd be scared to fool around with it. But five grains, and you cork off pretty.'

'Can you get it anywhere?' Mrs Morse felt superbly Machiavellian.

'Get all you want in Jersey,' said Mrs Miller. 'They won't give it to you here without you have a doctor's prescription. Finished? We'd better go back and see what the boys are doing.'

That night, Art left Mrs Morse at the door of her apartment; his mother was in town. Mrs Morse was still sober, and it happened that there was no whisky left in her cupboard. She lay in bed, looking up at the black ceiling.

She rose early, for her, and went to New Jersey. She had never taken the tube, and did not understand it. So she went to the Pennsylvania Station and bought a railroad ticket to Newark. She thought of nothing in particular on the trip out. She looked at the uninspired hats of the women about her and gazed through the smeared window at the flat, gritty scene.

In Newark, in the first drug-store she came to, she asked for a tin of talcum powder, a nailbrush, and a box of veronal tablets. The powder and the brush were to make the hypnotic seem also a casual need. The clerk was entirely unconcerned. 'We only keep them in bottles,' he said, and wrapped up for her a little glass vial containing ten white tablets, stacked one on another.

She went to another drug-store and bought a face-cloth, an orange-wood stick, and a bottle of veronal tablets. The clerk was also uninterested.

'Well, I guess I got enough to kill an ox,' she thought, and went back to the station.

At home, she put the little vials in the drawer of her dressing-table and stood looking at them with a dreamy tenderness.

'There they are, God bless them,' she said, and she kissed her finger-tip and touched each bottle.

The colored maid was busy in the living-room.

'Hey, Nettie,' Mrs Morse called. 'Be an angel, will you? Run around to Jimmy's and get me a quart of Scotch.'

She hummed while she awaited the girl's return.

During the next few days, whisky ministered to her as tenderly as it had done when she first turned to its aid. Alone, she was soothed and vague, at Jimmy's she was the gayest of the groups. Art was delighted with her.

Then, one night, she had an appointment to meet Art at Jimmy's for an early dinner. He was to leave afterward on a business excursion, to be away for a week. Mrs Morse had been drinking all the afternoon; while she dressed to go out, she felt herself rising pleasurably from drowsiness to high spirits. But as she came out into the street the effects of the whisky deserted her completely, and she was filled with a slow, grinding wretchedness so horrible that she stood swaying on the pavement, unable for a moment to move forward. It was a gray night with spurts of mean, thin snow, and the streets shone with dark ice. As she slowly crossed Sixth Avenue, consciously dragging one foot past the other, a big, scarred horse pulling a rickety express-wagon crashed to his knees before her. The driver swore and screamed and lashed the beast insanely, bringing the whip back over his shoulder for every blow, while the horse struggled to get a footing on the slippery asphalt. A group gathered and watched with interest.

Art was waiting, when Mrs Morse reached Jimmy's.

'What's the matter with you, for God's sake?' was his greeting to her.

'I saw a horse,' she said. 'Gee, I – a person feels sorry for horses. I – it isn't just horses. Everything's kind of terrible, isn't it? I can't help getting sunk.'

'Ah, sunk, me eye,' he said. 'What's the idea of all the belly-aching? What have you got to be sunk about?'

'I can't help it,' she said.

'Ah, help it, me eye,' he said. 'Pull yourself together, will you? Come on and sit down, and take that face off you.'

She drank industriously and she tried hard, but she could not overcome her melancholy. Others joined them and commented on her gloom, and she could do no more for them than smile weakly. She made little dabs at her eyes with her handkerchief, trying to time her movements so they would be unnoticed, but several times Art caught her and scowled and shifted impatiently in his chair.

When it was time for him to go to his train, she said she would leave, too, and go home.

'And not a bad idea, either,' he said. 'See if you can't sleep yourself out of it. I'll see you Thursday. For God's sake, try and cheer up by then, will you?'

'Yeah,' she said. 'I will.'

In her bedroom, she undressed with a tense speed wholly unlike her usual slow uncertainty. She put on her nightgown, took off her hair-net and passed the comb quickly through her dry, vari-colored hair. Then she took the two little vials from the drawer and carried them into the bathroom. The splintering misery had gone from her, and she felt the quick excitement of one who is about to receive an anticipated gift.

She uncorked the vials, filled a glass with water and stood before the mirror, a tablet between her fingers. Suddenly she bowed graciously to her reflection, and raised the glass to it.

'Well, here's mud in your eye,' she said.

The tablets were unpleasant to take, dry and powdery and sticking obstinately half-way down her throat. It took her a long time to swallow all twenty of them. She stood watching her reflection with deep, impersonal interest, studying the movements of the gulping throat. Once more she spoke aloud.

'For God's sake, try and cheer up by Thursday, will you?' she said. 'Well, you know what he can do. He and the whole lot of them.'

She had no idea how quickly to expect effect from the veronal. When she had taken the last tablet, she stood uncertainly, wondering, still with a courteous, vicarious interest, if death would strike her down then and there. She felt in no way strange, save for a slight stirring of sickness from the effort of swallowing the tablets, nor did her reflected face look at all different. It would not be immediate, then; it might even take an hour or so.

She stretched her arms high and gave a vast yawn.

'Guess I'll go to bed,' she said. 'Gee, I'm nearly dead.'

That struck her as comic, and she turned out the bathroom light and went in and laid herself down in her bed, chuckling softly all the time.

'Gee, I'm nearly dead,' she quoted. 'That's a hot one!'

III

Nettie, the colored maid, came in late the next afternoon to clean the apartment, and found Mrs Morse in her bed. But then, that was not unusual. Usually, though, the sounds of cleaning waked her, and she did not like to wake up. Nettie, an agreeable girl, had learned to move softly about her work.

But when she had done the living-room and stolen in to tidy the little square bedroom, she could not avoid a tiny clatter as she arranged the objects on the dressing-table. Instinctively, she glanced over her shoulder at the sleeper, and without warning a sickly uneasiness crept over her. She came to the bed and stared down at the woman lying there.

Mrs Morse lay on her back, one flabby, white arm flung up, the wrist against her forehead. Her stiff hair hung untenderly along her face. The bed covers were pushed down, exposing a deep square of soft neck and a pink nightgown, its fabric worn uneven by many launderings; her great breasts, freed from their tight confiner, sagged beneath her arm-pits. Now and then she made knotted, snoring sounds, and from the corner of her opened mouth to the blurred turn of her jaw ran a lane of crusted spittle.

'Mis' Morse,' Nettie called. 'Oh, Mis' Morse! It's terrible late.'

Mrs Morse made no move.

'Mis' Morse,' said Nettie. 'Look, Mis' Morse. How'm I goin' get this bed made?'

Panic sprang upon the girl. She shook the woman's hot shoulder.

'Ah, wake up, will yuh?' she whined. 'Ah, please wake up.'

Suddenly the girl turned and ran out in the hall to the elevator door, keeping her thumb firm on the black, shiny button until the elderly car and its Negro attendant stood before her. She poured a jumble of words over the boy, and led him back to the apartment. He tiptoed creakingly in to the bedside; first gingerly, then so lustily that he left marks in the soft flesh, he prodded the unconscious woman.

'Hey, there!' he cried, and listened intently, as for an echo.

'Jeez. Out like a light,' he commented.

At his interest in the spectacle, Nettie's panic left her. Importance was big in both of them. They talked in quick, unfinished whispers, and it was the boy's suggestion that he fetch the young doctor who lived on the ground floor. Nettie hurried along with him. They looked forward to the limelit moment of breaking their news of something untoward, something pleasurably unpleasant. Mrs Morse had become the medium of drama. With no ill wish to her, they hoped that her state was serious, that she would not let them down by being awake and normal on their return. A little fear of this determined them to make the most, to the doctor, of her present condition. 'Matter of life and death,' returned to Nettie from her thin store of reading. She considered startling the doctor with the phrase.

The doctor was in and none too pleased at interruption. He wore a yellow and blue striped dressing-gown, and he was lying on his sofa, laughing with a dark girl, her face scaly with inexpensive powder, who perched on the arm. Half-emptied highball glasses stood beside them, and her coat and hat were neatly hung up with the comfortable implication of a long stay. Always something, the doctor grumbled. Couldn't let anybody alone after a hard day. But he put some bottles and instruments into a case, changed his dressing-gown for his coat and started out with the Negroes.

'Snap it up there, big boy,' the girl called after him. 'Don't be all night.'

The doctor strode loudly into Mrs Morse's flat and on to the bedroom, Nettie and the boy right behind him. Mrs Morse had not moved; her sleep was as deep, but soundless, now. The doctor looked sharply at her, then plunged his thumbs into the lidded pits above her eyeballs and threw his weight upon them. A high, sickened cry broke from Nettie.

'Look like he tryin' to push her right on th'ough the bed,' said the boy. He chuckled.

Mrs Morse gave no sign under the pressure. Abruptly the doctor abandoned it, and with one quick movement swept the covers down to the foot of the bed. With another he flung her nightgown back and lifted the thick, white legs, cross-hatched with blocks of tiny, iris-colored veins. He pinched them repeatedly, with long, cruel nips, back of the knees. She did not awaken.

'What's she been drinking?' he asked Nettie, over his shoulder.

With the certain celerity of one who knows just where to lay hands on a thing, Nettie went into the bathroom, bound for the cupboard where Mrs Morse kept her whisky. But she stopped at the sight of the two vials, with their red and white labels, lying before the mirror. She brought them to the doctor.

'Oh, for the Lord Almighty's sweet sake!' he said. He dropped Mrs Morse's legs, and pushed them impatiently across the bed. 'What did she want to go taking that tripe for? Rotten yellow trick, that's what a thing like that is. Now we'll have to pump her out, and all that stuff. Nuisance, a thing like that is; that's what it amounts to. Here, George, take me down in the elevator. You wait here, maid. She won't do anything.'

'She won't die on me, will she?' cried Nettie.

'No,' said the doctor. 'God, no. You couldn't kill her with an ax.'

IV

After two days, Mrs Morse came back to consciousness, dazed at first, then with a comprehension that brought with it the slow, saturating wretchedness.

'Oh, Lord, oh, Lord,' she moaned, and tears for herself and for life striped her cheeks.

Nettie came in at the sound. For two days she had done the ugly, incessant tasks in the nursing of the unconscious, for two nights she had caught broken bits of sleep on the living-room couch. She looked coldly at the big, blown woman in the bed.

'What you been tryin' to do, Mis' Morse?' she said. 'What kine o' work is that, takin' all that stuff?'

'Oh, Lord,' moaned Mrs Morse, again, and she tried to cover

42

her eyes with her arms. But the joints felt stiff and brittle, and she cried out at their ache.

'Tha's no way to ack, takin' them pills,' said Nettie. 'You can thank you' stars you heah at all. How you feel now?'

'Oh, I feel great,' said Mrs Morse. 'Swell, I feel.'

Her hot, painful tears fell as if they would never stop.

'Tha's no way to take on, cryin' like that,' Nettie said. 'After what you done. The doctor, he says he could have you arrested, doin' a thing like that. He was fit to be tied, here.'

'Why couldn't he let me alone?' wailed Mrs Morse. 'Why the hell couldn't he have?'

'Tha's terr'ble, Mis' Morse, swearin' an' talkin' like that,' said Nettie, 'after what people done for you. Here I ain' had no sleep at all for two nights, an' had to give up goin' out to my other ladies!'

'Oh, I'm sorry, Nettie,' she said. 'You're a peach. I'm sorry I've given you so much trouble. I couldn't help it. I just got sunk. Didn't you ever feel like doing it? When everything looks just lousy to you?'

'I wouldn' think o' no such thing,' declared Nettie. 'You got to cheer up. Tha's what you got to do. Everybody's got their troubles.'

'Yeah,' said Mrs Morse. 'I know.'

'Come a pretty picture card for you,' Nettie said. 'Maybe that will cheer you up.'

She handed Mrs Morse a post-card. Mrs Morse had to cover one eye with her hand, in order to read the message; her eyes were not yet focusing correctly.

It was from Art. On the back of a view of the Detroit Athletic Club he had written: 'Greeting and salutations. Hope you have lost that gloom. Cheer up and don't take any rubber nickels. See you on Thursday.'

She dropped the card to the floor. Misery crushed her as if she were between great smooth stones. There passed before her a slow, slow pageant of days spent lying in her flat, of evenings at Jimmy's being a good sport, making herself laugh and coo at Art and other Arts; she saw a long parade of weary horses and shivering beggars and all beaten, driven, stumbling things. Her feet throbbed as if she had crammed them into the stubby champagne-colored slippers. Her heart seemed to swell and harden.

'Nettie,' she cried, 'for heaven's sake pour me a drink, will you?'

The maid looked doubtful.

'Now you know, Mis' Morse,' she said, 'you been near daid. I don' know if the doctor he let you drink nothin' yet.'

'Oh, never mind him,' she said. 'You get me one, and bring in the bottle. Take one yourself.'

'Well,' said Nettie.

She poured them each a drink, deferentially leaving hers in the bathroom to be taken in solitude, and brought Mrs Morse's glass in to her.

Mrs Morse looked into the liquor and shuddered back from its odor. Maybe it would help. Maybe, when you had been knocked cold for a few days, your very first drink would give you a lift. Maybe whisky would be her friend again. She prayed without addressing a God, without knowing a God. Oh, please, please, let her be able to get drunk, please keep her always drunk.

She lifted the glass.

'Thanks, Nettie,' she said. 'Here's mud in your eye.'

The maid giggled. 'That's the way, Mis' Morse,' she said. 'You cheer up, now.'

'Yeah,' said Mrs Morse. 'Sure.'

You Were Perfectly Fine

The pale young man eased himself carefully into the low chair, and rolled his head to the side, so that the cool chintz comforted his cheek and temple.

'Oh, dear,' he said. 'Oh, dear, oh, dear, oh, dear. Oh.'

The clear-eyed girl, sitting light and erect on the couch, smiled brightly at him.

'Not feeling so well today?' she said.

'Oh, I'm great,' he said. 'Corking, I am. Know what time I got up? Four o'clock this afternoon, sharp. I kept trying to make it, and every time I took my head off the pillow, it would roll under the bed. This isn't my head I've got on now. I think this is something that used to belong to Walt Whitman. Oh, dear, oh, dear, oh, dear.'

'Do you think maybe a drink would make you feel better?' she said.

'The hair of the mastiff that bit me?' he said. 'Oh, no, thank you. Please never speak of anything like that again. I'm through. I'm all, all through. Look at that hand; steady as a humming-bird. Tell me, was I very terrible last night?'

'Oh, goodness,' she said, 'everybody was feeling pretty high. You were all right.'

'Yeah,' he said. 'I must have been dandy. Is everybody sore at me?'

'Good heavens, no,' she said. 'Everyone thought you were terribly funny. Of course, Jim Pierson was a little stuffy, there, for a minute at dinner. But people sort of held him back in his chair, and got him calmed down. I don't think anybody at the other tables noticed it at all. Hardly anybody.'

'He was going to sock me?' he said. 'Oh, Lord. What did I do to him?'

'Why, you didn't do a thing,' she said. 'You were perfectly fine. But you know how silly Jim gets, when he thinks anybody is making too much fuss over Elinor.'

'Was I making a pass at Elinor?' he said. 'Did I do that?'

'Of course you didn't,' she said. 'You were only fooling, that's all. She thought you were awfully amusing. She was having a marvelous time. She only got a little tiny bit annoyed just once, when you poured the clam-juice down her back.'

'My God,' he said. 'Clam-juice down that back. And every vertebra a little Cabot. Dear God. What'll I ever do?'

'Oh, she'll be all right,' she said. 'Just send her some flowers, or something. Don't worry about it. It isn't anything.'

'No, I won't worry,' he said. 'I haven't got a care in the world. I'm sitting pretty. Oh, dear, oh, dear. Did I do any other fascinating tricks at dinner?'

'You were fine,' she said. 'Don't be so foolish about it. Everybody was crazy about you. The maître d'hôtel was a little worried because you wouldn't stop singing, but he really didn't mind. All he said was, he was afraid they'd close the place again, if there was so much noise. But he didn't care a bit, himself. I think he loved seeing you have such a good time. Oh, you were just singing away, there, for about an hour. It wasn't so terribly loud, at all.'

'So I sang,' he said. 'That must have been a treat. I sang.'

'Don't you remember?' she said. 'You just sang one song after another. Everybody in the place was listening. They loved it. Only you kept insisting that you wanted to sing some song about some kind of fusiliers or other, and everybody kept shushing you, and you'd keep trying to start it again. You were wonderful. We were all trying to make you stop singing for a minute, and eat something, but you wouldn't hear of it. My, you were funny.'

'Didn't I eat any dinner?' he said.

'Oh, not a thing,' she said. 'Every time the waiter would offer you something, you'd give it right back to him, because you said that he was your long-lost brother, changed in the cradle by a gypsy band, and that anything you had was his. You had him simply roaring at you.'

'I bet I did,' he said. 'I bet I was comical. Society's Pet, I must have been. And what happened then, after my overwhelming success with the waiter?'

'Why, nothing much,' she said. 'You took a sort of dislike to some old man with white hair, sitting across the room, because you didn't like his necktie and you wanted to tell him about it. But we got you out, before he got really mad.'

'Oh, we got out,' he said. 'Did I walk?'

'Walk! Of course you did,' she said. 'You were absolutely

all right. There was that nasty stretch of ice on the sidewalk, and you did sit down awfully hard, you poor dear. But good heavens, that might have happened to anybody.'

'Oh, sure,' he said. 'Louisa Alcott or anybody. So I fell down on the sidewalk. That would explain what's the matter with my – Yes, I see. And then what, if you don't mind?'

'Ah, now, Peter!' she said. 'You can't sit there and say you don't remember what happened after that! I did think that maybe you were just a little tight at dinner – oh, you were perfectly all right, and all that, but I did know you were feeling pretty gay. But you were so serious, from the time you fell down – I never knew you to be that way. Don't you know, how you told me I had never seen your real self before? Oh, Peter, I just couldn't bear it, if you didn't remember that lovely long ride we took together in the taxi! Please, you do remember that, don't you? I think it would simply kill me, if you didn't.'

'Oh, yes,' he said. 'Riding in the taxi. Oh, yes, sure. Pretty long ride, hmm?'

'Round and round and round the park,' she said. 'Oh, and the trees were shining so in the moonlight. And you said you never knew before that you really had a soul.'

'Yes,' he said. 'I said that. That was me.'

'You said such lovely, lovely things,' she said. 'And I'd never known, all this time, how you had been feeling about me, and I'd never dared to let you see how I felt about you. And then last night – oh, Peter dear, I think that taxi ride was the most important thing that ever happened to us in our lives.'

'Yes,' he said. 'I guess it must have been.'

'And we're going to be so happy,' she said. 'Oh, I just want to tell everybody! But I don't know – I think maybe it would be sweeter to keep it all to ourselves.'

'I think it would be,' he said.

'Isn't it lovely?' she said.

'Yes,' he said. 'Great.'

'Lovely!' she said.

'Look here,' he said, 'do you mind if I have a drink? I mean, just medicinally, you know I'm off the stuff for life, so help me. But I think I feel a collapse coming on.'

'Oh, I think it would do you good,' she said. 'You poor boy, it's a shame you feel so awful. I'll go make you a whisky and soda.'

'Honestly,' he said, 'I don't see how you could ever want to speak to me again, after I made such a fool of myself, last night. I think I'd better go join a monastery in Tibet.'

'You crazy idiot!' she said. 'As if I could ever let you go away now! Stop talking like that. You were perfectly fine.'

She jumped up from the couch, kissed him quickly on the forehead, and ran out of the room.

The pale young man looked after her and shook his head long and slowly, then dropped it in his damp and trembling hands.

'Oh, dear,' he said. 'Oh, dear, oh, dear, oh, dear.'